P9-DMV-323

Other Books by Natalie Savage Carlson

A BROTHER FOR THE ORPHELINES

CARNIVAL IN PARIS

THE FAMILY UNDER THE BRIDGE

THE HAPPY ORPHELINE

JEAN–CLAUDE'S ISLAND

THE LETTER ON THE TREE

THE ORPHELINES IN THE ENCHANTED CASTLE

A PET FOR THE ORPHELINES

SASHES RED AND BLUE

THE SONG OF THE LOP-EARED MULE

THE TALKING CAT

THE TOMAHAWK FAMILY

WINGS AGAINST THE WIND

HARPER & ROW, PUBLISHERS New York

The Empty Schoolhouse

by NATALIE SAVAGE CARLSON

Pictures by John Kaufmann

For Lydia Carlson

THE EMPTY SCHOOLHOUSE

Library of Congress Catalog Card Number: 65-11452

Contents

The Empty Schoolhouse

1

The Old Plantation

"Emma Royall," I always tell myself, "since you quit school in the sixth grade, you'll never be anything but a scrub girl at the Magnolia Motel."

But I got sick of being kept back so often. It seems like I never did have a head for books or a hankering to study.

For a while I was afraid that the truant officer would come after me. And if I'd been white, I reckon he would have.

It was different with Lullah. She's my little sister and she's real smart. She has always been promoted every year.

"I love spelling," she often says. And anybody who loves spelling has to be smart.

Lullah is the spittin' image of Mama and her kin. Her skin is like coffee and cream mixed together, and she has wavy hair to her shoulders. Me, I'm dark as Daddy Jobe and my hair never grew out much longer than he wears his.

Lullah was ten and I was fourteen the time I'm going to talk about. It was one of those hot summer days like we have in Louisiana. We were on our way to the ruins of the old Azalie plantation. I'd promised to take Lullah there to dig for the plantation treasure. Mama didn't want her to go alone because of the snakes in all that overgrown brush.

Little Jobe was dragging the shovel over the crushed white clamshells we call gravel on the side of the road. He was fooling along like five-year-olds do.

"Hurry up, Little Jobe," Lullah called to him. "You're always behind like a jaybird's tail."

Little Jobe looks like me and Daddy Jobe, but he's a handsome little boy all the same.

He grinned at Lullah and began showing off. " 'Member this and bear in mind, a jaybird's tail sticks out behind." He spoke the little singsong he'd learned from the older children.

"You play jaybird and you won't get to go digging the plantation treasure with me and Oralee," Lullah said to him.

She grabbed his hand and hustled him along. I knew what was her hurry. We were going to pick up Oralee Fleury at her house in French Grove on the way, and Lullah was afraid she'd go off somewhere else if we were late.

Oralee's a white girl. She's the same age as Lullah and goes to our church too. They're both in the same grade but had been in different schools. Oralee had been going to St. Joseph's School which was just for white children. And the public schools were segregated too, so Lullah had to go to the one for colored children.

But come fall, Lullah would get to go to St. Joseph's with Oralee because the Archbishop had made the rule that the parochial schools were to be open to all Catholic children no matter what their color.

Lullah and Oralee started playing together that summer when Mama was doing some sewing for Mrs. Fleury. And Lullah thought there was nobody else like Oralee.

"We got to hurry if we're going to find that treasure," Lullah said to Little Jobe as she pulled him along toward French Grove.

They say that way back in the War between the States the planter who owned Azalie gathered up all the family silver and jewels into a chest and gave it to a faithful old Negro slave to bury so the Yankees wouldn't get it. Then the old slave died before the war was over and nobody knew where he'd buried it. Ever since then folks have been digging off and on, but nobody's ever found the chest.

Lullah had been pestering me for a long time to go there with her so she could dig for it. So when I had a day off from the motel, I promised to take her. And right away she wanted to bring Oralee along.

And of course Little Jobe was so excited from hearing us talk about it that Mama made me take him too.

We walked along the road with the green sugarcane growing on both sides. We soon reached French Grove because we don't live far out. It's what they call a string village, because the houses are spread along the road for a long way. They're set up on concrete blocks and have big yards in front.

Little Jobe let go of Lullah's hand and came running to me.

"Perhaps somebody's already found the treasure," he said.

"No, it's still there," I told him. "A beautiful ghost lady in a hoop skirt came to me last night and told me so."

Little Jobe's eyes got big as if he was seeing her ghost too. Then he forgot about the lady in the hoop skirt because we were getting to the Superette General Store and Grocery. Mr. Cole, who owns it, was on the porch in front. He called out, "Howdy, children." We all said, "Howdy, Mr. Cole" back to him.

He's a friendly man and I like him. I often go to the superette for something or other. And he usually gives me something extra. He sells everything from harness to pickles so he does a good business.

Little Jobe loves that store, so he wanted to go in and look around.

"Remember what Mama told you," I reminded him. "She says don't you ever go in a store unless you got money in your pocket. It's just asking for temptation. A store's no place for a child without money."

"Anyway, we're in a hurry," Lullah said. "We've got no time to fool around in a store."

Oralee's house isn't far from the superette. It's a blue-and-white house shaded by magnolia trees. Two big holly bushes grow out front near the road.

We could see Oralee waiting on the front porch. She

ran down the steps waving both hands, and I thought she looked like a butterfly caught in the wind. She came skipping to meet us.

Oralee has big blue eyes and reddish hair she wears in a plait down her back. She always seemed like a butterfly to me because she's so pretty and flittery. But she's a nice little girl, so Mama liked to have Lullah play with her.

"I bet we're going to find that treasure for sure," she cried.

"Emma knows it's still there," Lullah said to her, "because the ghost of a beautiful lady in a hoop skirt came to her last night."

"You really saw a ghost?" Oralee asked, and her eyes got big as morning glories.

Of course I'd made up the whole thing for fun. But I said, "Uh-huh!" and looked wise as an old owl.

The road turns to the left past Oralee's house and goes on to Belltown, our nearest big town. The sugar fields along the road belong to Mr. Arnaud, the man Daddy Jobe works for.

It was a right good walk before we got to the long lane that leads into Azalie. All that's left of the big house are piles of broken bricks covered with vines and parts of the front pillars rotting into the ground. One of the dovecotes and the stack of the old sugarhouse are still standing. The brick slave quarters are down the hill and some of the workers live in them.

There are holes dug everywhere around the big old oak trees that used to shade the place. They were made by people hunting the treasure.

Right away I sat myself down on a chunk of pillar covered with moss. I just rested and listened to the mockingbirds singing in the oak trees.

Oralee and Lullah began arguing about where they were going to dig.

"Let me dig," Little Jobe kept whining at them. "I helped carry the shovel."

"You go play, boy," Lullah told him. "You're too little to dig with a big shovel."

"How come I'm too little to dig with it if I'm not too little to carry it?" Little Jobe wanted to know.

But Lullah didn't answer him. "If they never found the treasure here, maybe it's buried off in the garden," she said to Oralee.

"No, it isn't," I said. "That much the lady in the hoop skirt told me. She said it's buried near where the big house was."

I didn't want to have to chase snakes out of all those

weeds in the old garden. They say Azalie used to have the most beautiful azaleas in all the South, but you'd never know it now. The garden is like a jungle with everything gone wild.

So Oralee and Lullah took turns digging by one of the brick piles. Little Jobe amused himself pulling down the moss that hung on the trees. He twisted it around his head and let it hang down under his chin.

"Look, Lullah! Look, Oralee!" he called. "I'm an old man. I'm a real old man. Look, Emma! Everybody, look!"

He wasn't satisfied until we all looked at him and Lullah said, "Look at old Granddaddy Jobe. He's all shrunk up no bigger than Little Jobe Royall."

Little Jobe sure liked that.

At last the girls got hot and tired. The short hairs over Lullah's forehead were curled up like my own, and Oralee kept scratching the back of her neck under her plait.

Lullah threw herself on the ground to rest. "Here's the shovel, Little Jobe," she said. "You can dig with it all you want now."

Little Jobe's face was shining like a wet rock, but he grabbed the shovel and began trying to dig. It really was too big for him.

Oralee pulled up her skirt and sat down near Lullah.

"Let's play that Like Best game again," Lullah said to her. "What color you like best?"

"I like red because it's so bright and happy," Oralee answered.

"I like pink best," said Lullah. "It's half red but gentler."

"Me, I like yellow," I said, because I always have. I like yellow dresses and egg yolks and lemon pie and almost anything yellow.

"I like peppermint candy best," Little Jobe butted in.

We all had to break out laughing. That boy can come out with right comical things.

"What bird you like best?" Oralee took her turn.

"I like those pretty white egrets that fly around the swamps," Lullah said. "If I was a bird, I'd want to be an egret."

"I like the redbird," said Oralee, "and I reckon you know why."

Then Little Jobe said again, "I like peppermint candy best."

It wasn't funny anymore and Lullah was real put out with him. "Peppermint candy's not a bird either," she said to him. "What bird you like best, boy? Sparrow, mockingbird—"

"I like peppermint candy better'n colors or birds." Little Jobe stuck it out. He's stubborn as a pine tree growing through a rock, when he wants to be.

Lullah acted like she hadn't heard him right. "He says he likes the pelican best," she said to Oralee, "because it's got a big mouth like him."

But Little Jobe didn't pay her any mind because he'd gone back to wrestling with the shovel.

Then Oralee asked Lullah, "What friend you like best?"

"I like Oralee Fleury best," Lullah said.

"And I like Lullah Royall," said Oralee. "She's my best friend."

About then Little Jobe started hollering, "I found it! I found the treasure!"

He dropped the shovel and began clawing in the dirt. Then he came running to me with something in his fist. The girls jumped up and came over to see what it was.

"It's just an old bottle top or something," Lullah said.

But when I wiped it off, I saw it was a quarter. "It's got 1926 on it," I said. "It must be the plantation treasure if it's that old."

Those children were just as happy as if Little Jobe had dug up a chest of silver and jewels.

He put the quarter in his pocket and said, "Now I got money in my pocket so I can go in the store on the way home and buy us all some peppermint candy."

Then we really had to laugh. The joke sure was on us.

The children had a real good time that day at Azalie, and Lullah made me promise to take them there again.

2

Mr. Buzzard and Mr. 'Gator

Somehow the summer flitted by so fast that we never did get back to Azalie. First thing we knew it was time to think about Lullah's school. Mama had already registered her at St. Joseph's.

"When do you reckon it'll open?" Lullah kept asking.

"I don't know," Mama would say, "and I'm not going to ask Father Austin. Just be patient. You'll find out in time, that's sure."

Mama is a quiet, proud woman.

"You must really be an Indian, Rose," Daddy Jobe says when he wants to tease her. "You've got such a tight mouth and poker backbone."

Mama walks real straight as if she's carrying a basket on her head all the time. But when she does talk, she means business.

"Then you must be a turkey," Mama teases him back. "You talk so gobbly."

Daddy Jobe does talk deep down in his throat, but there's music in it like the notes of a bass fiddle. And for such a big, strong man he's gentle as a bird dog's mouth.

On Sunday we always go to the seven o'clock mass at St. Joseph's because I have to work that day. Weekends are busy at a motel.

We get up early and bring in water from the cistern beside the cabin. It's a big wooden barrel on stilts, and it catches the rainwater we use for washing and cooking. Our cabin is moss-gray with a tin roof. And a trumpet vine grows over the porch.

Daddy Jobe drives us to church in the third-hand car he uses for going back and forth to the cane fields on workdays. Sometimes it's hard to get started, but that Sunday morning toward the end of August it took right off.

We went into the church and sat down in back with the rest of the colored folks. Daddy Jobe and Mama pulled Little Jobe in between them because he fidgets so.

Father Austin said the mass. He's a little short man with a bald head, but when he gets up in the pulpit he looks tall. And when he begins talking, seems like he's even taller.

He started out with the announcements. "St. Joseph's School will open the fourth of September," he began. "All parents who haven't done so are urged to register their children as soon as possible. We expect a larger enrollment this year because of the new Negro pupils."

He said it as natural as if he was talking about the time of confessions or where the sodality would meet. But I could feel Lullah's shoulder jerk. We were that tight in the pew. Mama looked at her and smiled as if to say, "I told you so."

Little Jobe clapped his hands and said out loud, "Good!"

Daddy Jobe grabbed his hands and Mama put her fingers over his mouth. Some of the folks around us giggled.

Lullah started squirming around trying to see if Oralee was up front. But Mama gave her a little shake.

Then Father Austin began reading the gospel and we all stood up. I saw Oralee's straw hat with the red poppies on it rise up among the first. She turned around looking for Lullah, but Mrs. Fleury jerked her back.

"I can't abide children turning around and staring at the people behind them in church," Mrs. Fleury once said to Mama.

And Mama said, "That's right. Only thing worse is grown-ups turning around and frowning at little babies that fret."

After he had finished the gospel, Father Austin began the sermon. He talked about the commandment "Love thy neighbor."

"If there's one thing in which we citizens of French Grove can take pride," he said, "it's in the way we have always lived and worked together in peace and goodwill."

Since the colored folks sit in back of the church, they get out first. Some of them hurried on home. And those that stayed around acted kind of shy.

But most of the white people seemed the same as ever. Mrs. Cole, the storekeeper's wife, said to me, "I reckon you'll be going back to school now, Emma."

I shook my head and told her, "No, ma'am. I've been out a year and I'm used to making my own money. Seems like once you're done with school, you're done for good."

By that time Lullah spotted Oralee in the crowd, and those two were excited as hound dogs under a treed possum.

"Come around and I'll show you the school," Oralee told Lullah. "You come too, Emma, and see our school."

Little Jobe started to follow us, but Mama grabbed him. "You stay right here where I can keep an eye on you," she said. "You'll see inside a school sooner than you want."

We passed a bunch of white women talking apart from the others. Mrs. Tessin was one of them, and I heard her say, "I'm not sending my children back to St. Joseph's, I can tell you."

Mrs. Turnbuckle looked over her shoulder and saw us, so she said in a real low voice, "Don't worry. My husband's seeing to it that we get some outside help."

I've got ears sharp as a bat's, but what she said didn't bother me any because I thought maybe she meant they were going to get more teachers for the public school.

St. Joseph's School is a fine brick building. It's two stories high with great big windows and a flat roof that sticks out over the walk. There are chinaberry trees on the grounds, and the oleander bushes along the walls were full of pink flowers.

First Oralee tried the main door under the statue of St. Joseph, then the side ones. "They're all locked," she said in a disappointed voice.

I looked through a window that was low, but all I could see was a stairway going up.

Oralee backed away and pointed. "The fifth grade is up there. Those two—three—four windows at the corner. That's where we'll be. We'll go in the door on this side and hang our coats and things in the girls' cloakroom. It's got mirrors and washbasins. We'll walk—no running in the halls—up the steps to our room and take our places when the bell rings. Then Sister Rosalie will pass out the books and paper. She wears glasses and she's real strict, but everybody likes her."

Lullah kept nodding her head all the time, and her eyes were shining like lightning bugs.

She looked like Oralee was saying to her, "And this is the pearly gate to heaven. We'll hang up our halos in the cloakroom and walk up the golden stairs to the fifth grade room. Then we'll sit down on a cloud and wait for them to bring us our harps."

That's the way it must have sounded to my little sister.

They kept hanging around the school, so I had to leave

them. I'd promised Mrs. Lepine to be at the motel by eight thirty to get the place cleaned up. We'd had a full house over the weekend so there would be plenty of muss and dirt.

It wasn't a long walk to the main highway where the motel is, so I didn't want Daddy Jobe to waste his gas driving me there. Besides, he and Mama were talking to some of the friends they only get to see on Sunday.

Mrs. Lepine sure was glad to see me. She's a driving woman with a sharp tongue, but she's always been fair to me.

"That crowd in Sixteen made a mess out of the place," she said. "The hot water faucet left running and cigarette ashes all over the carpet."

"We get a lot of folks like that," I reminded her, "and I wonder what their own home looks like if they throw their trash all over the floor and wipe off their shoes on the towels."

I took off my Sunday hat and changed fast into the old dress and apron I keep in the service closet. I tied a black scarf around my head like Mama does to keep out the dust. Only I just twist the ends of mine under, but Mama ties hers into a butterfly bow over her forehead. An old time *tignon*, she calls it.

I filled the bucket with water and detergent and

slopped the mop into it. First I went from one room to the other, mopping the bathroom floors while Mrs. Lepine carried out the dirty laundry.

"Emma Royall," I often tell myself, "if you were a teacher or stenographer, you'd want to be the best. So since you can't be them, you'll just have to try to be the best scrub girl there is."

And Mrs. Lepine says I am. She scolds me if I'm late or miss some places dusting, but she's ready to say nobody can scrub clean as I do.

I was trying to do extra good on the cement walk that runs in front of all the doors. A motorist sees that before he does the bathroom, so I wanted it to look like we were running a real clean motel.

I was down on my hands and knees using a rag on some gritty places when I heard a car pull in. I looked up and saw Mrs. Lepine with her keys in her hand bringing a man over.

"Number Twelve is the only one half ready," she was telling him. "It's so early that the beds haven't been made yet."

"That's okay," he said. "We're just over here to shoot crows so we ain't choosy."

As he came closer I could see he was flat-headed

with a red face and a long neck. Right off I called him Mr. Buzzard to myself.

Then an old green car with a Mississippi license plate chugged over and parked at the curb. Another man got out and followed them into Number Twelve. He had a lumpy nose and puffy eyes. His top teeth poked over his bottom lip like an alligator's so I named him Mr. 'Gator.

I never did see two such ugly men.

They began unloading, and one of them carried a gun case into the room. But by the time I reached the front of Number Twelve with my mop, I'd almost forgotten there was anybody in the motel yet.

Suddenly the door opened and Mr. Buzzard came out so fast he pretty near fell over the scrub bucket. He pulled back his foot and gave it such a kick it almost upset, and the water sloshed all over my legs.

"Get that stuff out of my way, nigger," he yelled at me.

I felt like he'd kicked me instead of the bucket. I was so mad I wanted to yank the mop out of the bucket and slap it across his face. And I think I would have if it hadn't been Sunday.

We didn't see much more of those men at the motel. They slept there but they were gone all day.

Next afternoon when I dropped in the superette to get cornmeal for Mama on the way home from work, I saw old Mr. Buzzard buying some tobacco.

There were lots of women in the store at that time because they were buying the food they needed for supper.

Mr. Buzzard looked around and said, "I reckon there'll be fireworks in this town pretty soon."

Mr. Cole looked at him surprised like. "We won't be setting off fireworks until Christmas," he said.

Mr. Buzzard laughed like an old crow cawing. "I didn't mean that," he said. "I mean about letting all the niggers into your church school."

A couple of women stopped talking and stared at him.

Then the storekeeper said, "We may not all be in favor, mister, but we're law-abiding people here in French Grove. We don't expect any trouble."

"I don't know," Mr. Buzzard went on. "There's been plenty of trouble in other places. Bombs in schools and screaming mobs let loose."

"That's other places," Mr. Cole said, "and this is French Grove."

Mr. Buzzard picked at his teeth. "I'm just warning you," he said. "I was talking to some big boys out in the field where I was hunting. They said a lot of folks are riled up and there'll probably be trouble on opening day." He looked around at the women. "Wouldn't want to see little children hurt."

Then he picked up his change from the tobacco and shuffled out.

Seemed like the store was quiet as a church after that. I felt uncomfortable the rest of the time I was in there buying the cornmeal—like I was walking on spilled sugar.

3

The Opening of School

The Sunday before school opened, Father Austin laid down some rules from the pulpit.

"After the eight o'clock mass," he said, "all the pupils will immediately enter the school. There is to be no loitering. And no adults are to be on the school grounds. I hope I have made that clear."

It was clear as spring water to me. He must have heard about what Mr. Buzzard had said in the store, and he didn't want any trouble around the school after the daily mass.

"You won't be the only new one at St. Joseph's," Mama told Lullah. "Some of the other children from your old school will be going too. Lizzie Tucker put in her Charlie's name, and Irma Roche her two the day I was there."

I piped up and said, "I heard Mrs. Aubert at the superette saying she's not sending Stella and Leon until she sees it's safe. Do you think we ought to let Lullah go first thing off?"

Mama gave me a look that would freeze a boiling kettle. "If everybody is scared off by talk," she said, "there won't be any school."

"I'm not afraid, Mama," Lullah said. "Not as long as Oralee is there with me. Everything will be all right."

One night a little before school opened, Daddy Jobe came home from work real worried.

"They say there's going to be a mob at the school opening day," he told Mama. "Maybe we better let Lullah wait home until things quiet down."

Mama was put out with him. "Talk, talk, talk," she said. "Some stranger in the store says maybe there'll be trouble when school opens. Then right off everybody starts talking themselves into it."

Daddy Jobe just kept shaking his head slowly as if he didn't see it the same way as Mama, but he didn't say anything more.

Lullah didn't pay much attention to either of them. She was more interested in what she was going to wear to school that first day. It was still hot as blazes, but she was bound to wear the new blue wool dress Mama had made for her.

"You'll roast in that," Mama said.

"No, I won't," Lullah said. "I'll leave off some of my underwear."

The day before school opened, Daddy Jobe said, "I'll take Lullah to school. I'll ask Mr. Arnaud for part of the morning off. You stay home with Little Jobe, Rose. We wouldn't want him mixed up in any trouble." Mama gave him such a sharp look that he went on, "If there *is* any trouble."

Little Jobe began begging, "I want to see the trouble. I want to bring Lullah to school and see the trouble."

That boy can be bothersome as a chinch bug sometimes. Mama gave him a slap.

"Now see what you've done." she said to Daddy. "You've got him all stirred up. You'll stay home with me, boy," she told Little Jobe. "There's not going to be any trouble, so there's no use in us going to see it. But if you're good, you can go to meet Lullah when school's out."

The way it ended up, Daddy Jobe was going to drive me and Lullah to school on his way to work, and we'd wait around to see that she got in all right. Then I'd walk on to the motel.

But the next morning was one that he couldn't get the car started. We kept hanging around waiting for it to catch. At last Daddy Jobe said, "It's getting late. You girls better start walking and I'll catch up with you on the road or in town."

He never did catch up with us and we got into French Grove alone. I said to Lullah, "No matter what happens, play like you're taking part in a show. You just go ahead like you're supposed to do. Remember that time we had the Christmas play at the colored school? And the big boys came and hooted at us because we were wearing our long white nightgowns, and our paper wings hung crooked? We just went on with our acting like they weren't even there."

Lullah squeezed my hand and looked around for Daddy Jobe. I know she was a little scared by then.

When we reached St. Joseph's, I could see we were too late for mass. It was out and there was a crowd of white folks gathered in front of the school. My heart turned a somersault. I was tempted to turn Lullah around and march her home.

Then I saw that the crowd was mostly parents who were probably worried about their own children, although some of them looked mad.

When we got closer, I heard a couple grumbling about

the Archbishop's new rule. Then Mrs. Turnbuckle said, "There wouldn't be all this violence if they'd stayed in their own school." A lady next to her must have been something like Mama because she asked, "All *what* violence?"

"You'll see," Mrs. Turnbuckle answered her.

There were some big white boys who started saying pert things.

"Now ain't we all dressed up pretty?" one of them said, looking at Lullah's new blue dress. He began mincing around on his toes, making fun of her.

"The bottom rail sure has come to the top," said another.

Daddy Jobe still hadn't come, so Lullah and I began looking around for Oralee, but she must have gone in already. And we didn't see any of the colored children.

"You better go right in," I told Lullah. "Remember what Father Austin said in church."

Then some of the big boys edged up closer to us. Lullah squeezed my hand tighter—as if she didn't want to let go. "Can't you just come to the door with me, Emma?" she begged. "You're not a grown-up."

I said to her, "Seems like you can do that much by yourself because you've always had things made easy for you, and it's been different with me."

She looked real surprised and said, "But, Emma, you're lucky to be the oldest one so you can work and make a lot of money all your own."

"Uh-huh," I answered her. "I make it by the sweat of my brow—like it says in the Bible—and it's not a lot. You walk into that school and get a good education, and you won't have to sweat so hard." Then I let go of her hand and gave her a good push like we always did the ones who were stage-scared in the school plays.

A low buzzing went through the little crowd as Lullah started down the walk toward the school door. The big boys began whistling and making catcalls. They really weren't acting much different from the ones who yelled at us during the Christmas play, but these were white boys, so it gave me the shivers.

Suddenly I saw something nearly scared me frozen. Mr. Buzzard was walking across the school yard from the side. He was walking straight to Lullah. I saw her tremble and slow down.

Mr. Buzzard stopped on the walk and blocked her. Lullah stopped dead too. Then she raised her head and walked straight at him. I thought she was going to bump right into him but he stepped aside. It looked like he said something to her. But Lullah kept right on walking. A few more steps and she was safe inside the door.

Then Father Austin must have finished taking off his vestments because he came out of the side door of the church. At sight of him, Mr. Buzzard slunk away.

Soon some of the colored children came with their parents. They live way out in the country, so I reckon they couldn't get there in time for mass either.

Those little children were just stiff with starch and pride. They went marching so proudfully into the school. The big boys hooted at them too, until Father Austin started down the walk toward them. Then they ran away.

The crowd quickly broke up, and about that time Daddy Jobe got there all out of breath. "Is she in safe?" he asked me.

"Uh-huh," I told him. "Wasn't really any trouble after all. Just a smarty man wanted to start something but he didn't get far. But you're on foot. Where's the car?"

"It never did start," he said. "The battery wore down to the last, so now we both have to walk to work."

When I got to the Magnolia, Mrs. Lepine said the two hunters in Number Twelve had just checked out. "Good riddance to bad rubbish," I thought to myself.

I sure was anxious to get home and hear all about Lullah's first day at school.

"It was real quiet there except for the children,"

Mama said. "I told you there wouldn't be any trouble."

Lullah was just popping with news to tell me.

"Some of the girls like Shirley Benoit and Myrtle Turnbuckle wouldn't have anything to do with me," she said, "but they weren't the ones who mattered. And you know what? Sister Rosalie made me and Oralee monitors for the week. We get to clean the boards and empty the trash baskets."

"That's fine," Mama spoke up. "Maybe you'd like to be the monitor more around here."

"But that mean man in the school yard this morning?" I asked Lullah. "What did he say to you?"

Her eyes got big and frightened. "He hissed at me like a snake," she said. "He just hissed, 's-s-s-s.' I was powerful scared, and I was going to turn around and run. But I remembered what you said, Emma. I played like I was a beautiful angel with wings like an egret. And couldn't anybody hurt an angel—even that bad man."

"You and the crows don't have to worry about him anymore," I said. "He and old Mr. 'Gator have gone on. They checked out at the motel this morning."

"I'm proud of you, Lullah," Mama said. "I've always been proud of my children, but now I've got a good reason."

4

Little Jobe Visits School

Lullah was happy as a little tree frog in the rain over going to St. Joseph's. And deep down I was really envious of her as an old toad down in the mud. Specially since I hadn't done so well in school myself.

"And you know what Sister Rosalie did at recess this morning?" she said to Mama the next day. "Some of us girls were standing around together and she came over and joked with us. She's full of fun outside the classroom—but not in it. And before she left us, she pinched my nose. Out of all those girls standing there and most of them white, it was my nose she pinched."

Lullah was proud as if Sister Rosalie had pinned a gold medal on her.

Little Jobe listened to her, all eyes and ears.

"I want to go to St. Joseph's," he said. "When can I go?"

"It'll be another year yet," Mama told him.

"Maybe he could come visit my room," Lullah said. "I'll ask Sister Rosalie if it's all right."

First Mama was against it. "He'd have to be there all day with you unless I pick him up noontime," she said to Lullah. "And you know Little Jobe can't keep quiet and good very long."

"But I'll ask Sister Rosalie," Lullah kept on. "I wish he could see my school."

She did ask about it, and Sister Rosalie sure enough told her she could bring her little brother to visit school the next day.

"She said he can even stay all day so he can eat lunch with us," Lullah said.

It was during supper that Mama said to Daddy Jobe, "Jobe, poor Irma Roche must be real lonesome these evenings with her husband working overtime getting the mill machinery ready for harvest. Why don't we drop down the road to see her awhile after the dishes are done. We won't stay long."

"I'll go, too," I said, "since you're not staying late."

Lullah couldn't go because she had homework. So that meant she could put Little Jobe to bed early since he'd have to get up early next morning to go to school with her.

It was a pretty sunset ahead of us when we walked down the road to the Roches'. Half the sky was yellow, and you know how I love that color. Even the cane looked golden instead of green. But right where the sun was going down, it was all pink like Lullah loves.

Mrs. Roche really was glad to see us.

"Harvest time is good some ways," she said, "but bad others. George makes more money but he hardly gets home at all—even before it really starts."

Velma and Georgie Roche were busy with their homework. They hardly took time off to tell us all "Howdy."

Daddy Jobe doesn't care much for going visiting when the man is away and there are just women, but he sat real polite-like and looked at the new green dress Mrs. Roche was sewing on.

"It's mighty pretty," he said. "Maybe you ought to make one just like it, Rose."

Then when Mama was telling Mrs. Roche how to cook a vegetable gumbo for Friday, he said, "Maybe you could sneak in a little bacon grease to give it some taste. And if I was cooking it, I'd leave out the red pepper."

Yes, Daddy Jobe sure was polite and talkative even if Mr. Roche wasn't there.

Everything was going so quiet and peaceful. There was only the sound of our voices and the scratching of the children's pencils.

I had just started telling about the diamond earrings Mrs. Lepine bought in Belltown for two dollars when we heard a screeching outside like tomcats fighting.

Daddy Jobe got up to look out the window, but before he could get to it, there was an awful crash. Broken glass flew all over the floor and something hard hit against the wall, just missing Georgie's head.

Daddy jumped back just in time. First I thought the outside gas tank for the stove had exploded or a tornado had hit.

We were so shocked we stared at each other like strange cats for a couple of seconds.

Then Mrs. Roche screamed, "It's a bomb! It's going to blow up!"

Daddy almost knocked me down to rush to the thing that had come through the window and get rid of it. When he held it up I could see his hand trembled a little.

"It's just—just a rock," he told us. And I could hear his voice trembled too, but he was trying to keep us from being so scared.

Velma began bawling, "They're going to kill us." By then she had crawled under the table.

"I don't want to get killed," Little Georgie began howling. "I'm getting out of here."

He started for the back door but Daddy caught him by the shirttail.

"It's only a rock, Georgie," he said to him. "There's lots of them on the road." But Daddy Jobe knew that rock was a heap different from the ones on the road. He quickly said to Mrs. Roche, "Shut off the lights."

Then he opened the door and looked out. "It's so black I can't see anything," he said, "but I can hear rustling through the cane. They must be in there."

"Why would anybody want to throw a rock through our window?" Mrs. Roche asked in a shaky voice. "George never has quarreled with anybody."

"It's that school trouble," Daddy Jobe said. "That's what it is."

Then Mama cried out in such a scared voice for her, "Lullah and Little Jobe! They're all alone at home. We've got to go."

"We can't leave Irma and her family alone," Daddy said.

"But what about our children?" cried Mama. "There's nobody with them. Emma and me can go back together."

"No, you can't," Daddy said. "I won't let you two out on the road unprotected."

And I'm ashamed to say I was real glad about that.

The way it ended, the whole bunch of us went to our cabin together. The pretty yellow sunset was gone. The sky was dark and the new moon sharp as a cat's claw. The white gravel made the road look like a ghost trail through the jungle of black cane. Then the whippoorwills began calling from the woods behind the cane fields like they were warning us.

We tiptoed down the middle of the road, talking in whispers. Even the children were scared quiet.

Everything was all right at our house. Lullah had put Little Jobe to sleep and laid out his good clothes for school. And she was sound asleep herself.

We didn't wake her. Just began putting the Roche children to sleep in my bed.

"I'm going to the mill to get George," Daddy Jobe told Mrs. Roche.

"No, no," Mama cried. "Don't go out in that black night all by yourself."

"Wait until morning," Mrs. Roche said.

"No, I got to go right away," Daddy Jobe kept on. "I got to warn him because they might be waiting in the cane for him."

Nothing they said could change him, so soon as he was out the door we all knelt down and prayed he would be safe. We said all the regular prayers, then Mama began talking straight to God. She seemed to be looking clear up through the roof when she said to Him, "You watch over the sparrows and the cane and the weather, so please watch out for Jobe and George."

And He did. Because they both got back safe and Mr. Roche gathered up his brood and went home. And no more rocks came through their window—or ours either.

My eyes sure were half shut the next morning. But the first thing I saw when I got them open was Little Jobe up and dressed for school by himself. His shoes were on the wrong feet, so he looked like he was walking off two different ways.

At first Mama and Daddy Jobe didn't want Lullah going to school that day because of what had happened at the Roches'.

"You just stay home, honey, and have a holiday today," Daddy told her.

"I don't want a holiday," Little Jobe bawled. "All the time I have holidays and now I want to go to school with Lullah."

"You can go tomorrow or the next day," Mama said to him.

"Lullah said today I was to go to school with her," he kept on. "And I'm all dressed by myself and ready."

Mama and Daddy Jobe sure had picked the wrong day to try to keep Lullah home when Little Jobe was aiming to go with her.

"I reckon they might as well be in school as here," Daddy finally said.

So Little Jobe got his way like he usually does.

"You be a good boy and listen to Lullah," Mama told him as they left. "And be polite to the sisters. And both of you come straight home when school's out," she told Lullah.

Since I could see Mama was worried, I decided to take a holiday myself and keep her company. The middle of the week isn't very busy at a motel anyhow.

Mama fretted around all day over how Little Jobe was behaving himself at school. But I knew she was really worried that somebody might hurt him or Lullah.

"I hope he doesn't pester Sister Rosalie like he did us about school today," she said, "and I hope he and Lullah don't have to sit too near a window. Might be drafty there."

She'd keep looking at the clock and saying, "They must be eating lunch now. I hope Little Jobe puts on his good manners." Then around three she said, "Let's walk down the road and meet them, Emma. I'd like to hear about how Little Jobe made out."

So I walked down the road with her and we met them near the Legrands' cane field. Little Jobe's hands were full of holy cards the sisters gave him.

Lullah was proud as a peahen. "He told everybody along the way that he was taking me to school," Lullah said.

"I was a good boy," Little Jobe bragged. "Sister Rosalie said I was a good boy."

"You wouldn't even know it was Little Jobe." Lullah backed him up. "Sister let him draw with chalk on one part of the blackboard. And she gave him books to look at. And she had me take him down to the first grade and let him pick out the seat he wants when he starts school."

"There was a boy in my seat," said Little Jobe. "When's that boy going to get out of my seat?"

"Just one more year before that seat's empty," said Mama, "and I'd sure like to see you stay good that long."

The very next morning when we got up, we found Little Jobe all dressed again, only this time he had forgotten to put on his underwear, and he didn't have his shoes on because he couldn't find them in the dark.

"I'm all ready to bring Lullah to school again," he told Mama.

He sure was broken up when he found out he couldn't.

"You have to wait another year like I told you," Mama said.

Lullah had a better reason. "You've got to wait until that boy gets out of your seat," she said to him. "I'll keep watch and let you know when."

5

The Empty Schoolhouse

The Roches quit sending their children to school soon after the rock came through the window.

Lullah kind of missed Velma because they had been in the same grade in public school too.

Then the Benoits took Shirley out because somebody called Mr. Benoit up and said he'd lose his job if his daughter kept on going to that school with nigger children.

Lullah was doing fine at St. Joseph's, and she sure liked it there. That's why Mama and Daddy Jobe didn't stop her going. But one day she came home early without any books. It was my day off but no school holiday.

"How come you're out at this time?" Mama asked. "It's no holy day."

"Everybody got sent home early," Lullah told her. "Somebody called up the rectory and said there was a bomb in the school."

"Glory be!" cried Mama.

We were glad that Little Jobe was playing in the kitchen. I peeked in and he was busy making a face on a paper bag so I was content he couldn't hear what we were talking about.

"Father Austin came right over and told everybody to clear the rooms right away," Lullah went on. "We stood out on the playground while he and the janitor went all through the school looking for the bomb."

"Did they get it?" Mama wanted to know.

"No," Lullah said. "They couldn't find anything. Father sent us home anyhow because some of the children were crying and Myrtle Turnbuckle got hysterics."

Right then there was a big *BANG* behind Mama. She jumped up in the air, Lullah screamed, and I almost fainted.

"Bomb, bomb, bomb!" Little Jobe half sang. "Bang, bang, bang!"

He had blown up that sack and popped it behind

Mama. She grabbed him and gave him such a slapping that he began singing a different tune.

When Daddy Jobe heard about the bomb scare at school, he was as upset as we had been by the rock that came through the Roches' window.

"We better do like the Roches and take Lullah out of that school," he said.

Then Lullah began crying, "I want to go to St. Joseph's. Oralee, she's still going. I want to go to school with her."

Mama stood there a little while twisting her apron. Then she turned to Lullah. "You're not afraid, girl?" she asked. "Could be one day there'll be a real bomb in that school."

"I don't care," Lullah sobbed. "I want to go. I wasn't one of the crying ones. And Oralee and I get to read a poem together in front of the class tomorrow. We take turns with each stanza."

Mama thought it over. Then she let loose of her apron and said, "Then you better go back and read the poem."

So Lullah went back, but some more of the children stayed away. There had been more phone calls with threats that some father would lose his job or a bomb would be thrown into his house.

Lullah didn't worry as long as Oralee stayed in school. But it sure bothered Mama and Daddy Jobe.

"I feel better we don't have a phone for them to call me," Daddy said.

One day Lullah came home later than usual.

"What are you dragging your feet about?" Mama asked her.

"Oralee's quit St. Joseph's," she said. "I thought she was sick and that's why she was absent. So I went to her house after school to tell her what the lessons would be for tomorrow. Then Mrs. Fleury told me she's sending Oralee to the public school."

Lullah didn't do her homework that night. She just moped around. The next night she said to Mama, "I'm going back to the colored school. It's too lonesome at St. Joseph's without Oralee and the rest. It just makes me feel sad and I can't study."

"You're the one to decide," Mama said. "We'll have to get your transfer from St. Joseph's."

But Little Jobe sure set up a squawk when he found out.

"You said you'd let me know when that boy gets out of my seat," he cried to Lullah. "If you stop school, I can't ever go."

"You can go to the old school with me," Lullah said.

"I don't want to go there," whined Little Jobe. "I got my seat picked out at St. Joseph's, and Sister Rosalie said I was to sit there."

But it wouldn't have made any difference in the long run, because more and more parents took their children out of St. Joseph's School. So we saw fewer and fewer children going through that door Oralee had pointed out to Lullah before school even started. Pretty soon the school was empty.

"Our school will not be closed," Father Austin said from the pulpit. "Every weekday morning I shall unlock the door and the sisters will enter and go to their classrooms. Whether your children attend or not is your responsibility from there on."

And that's the way it was.

I saw the school get opened one morning when I was taking a shortcut that way.

It looked so lonesome. The leaves on the chinaberry trees had turned yellow and were slowly falling to the ground. The flowers were gone from the oleander bushes. And those big windows looked even emptier than during summer vacation.

Then Father Austin came marching along the walk

from the church. He went to the main door and unlocked it. He turned and looked across the street.

The sisters followed from the convent like a flock of blackbirds. I figured Sister Rosalie was the one wearing glasses.

There was nobody around but me because early mass had let out. And I scooted off before one of them could get the notion to talk me into going back to school.

It seemed like lots of white people weren't as nice to us as they used to be. They never had mixed with us, but they had always given us a "Good morning" or "How's everything with your family?" Now most of them began acting like we had the smallpox or something.

One day I met up with my special friend Eula Mae Tucker when she was on her way to Uncle Vounie's. He's the old remedy man lives back in the swamp with the alligators. He makes medicine for sick folks, and Eula Mae gets root tea from him for her old grandmother who's full of coughs and mumbles. But some of the children run when they see him coming because they think he's a hoodoo man and that he'll put a spell on them.

We walked along, and car after car of white people we knew passed by. But none of them stopped to offer us a lift like they often do.

"It's all their fault," I heard Mrs. Tessin say real loud in the superette, as if she wanted me to hear. "They weren't satisfied with their own school and now they've closed up ours."

"Looks to me like the school's open," Mr. Cole said, "but the parents just aren't sending their children."

He was one of the few whites who wasn't mad at us.

When I told Daddy Jobe and Mama, Daddy said, "Seems to me they're just looking for a scrapegoat to scrape off their fear on. And it's us they've picked."

Lullah wasn't seeing so much of Oralee any more.

"She plays with Lily Michot," Lullah said, "because now they're both going to school together. Lily's always gone to the public school."

"Then why don't you go see Oralee some Saturday when she's not in school?" Mama said.

My two weeks' vacation I get in the fall had started by

the next Saturday. I was going to walk into town and meet Eula Mae Tucker at the bus stop for Belltown. We could go there and maybe see a movie.

So I said to Lullah, "You want to walk in with me and keep me company on the way, and I'll take you by Oralee's?"

The walk seems to go faster if you've got somebody to talk to. So it didn't seem any time until we reached the Fleurys'.

It was all quiet with no sign of Oralee outside. We went to the back door and knocked. Mrs. Fleury opened it, untying her apron real fast because she didn't know it was us.

"Is Oralee home, ma'am, and can she come out and play with me?" asked Lullah.

"She isn't here," Mrs. Fleury told her, beginning to tie her apron strings. "She and Lily Michot went to the school grounds to play. Why don't you go and look for them there? I'm sure they'll be glad to play with you."

"St. Joseph's school yard?" Lullah asked.

"No, the public school where they go," Mrs. Fleury said.

I went on to the public school with Lullah because it was on my way. I could see something was bothering her. When we were almost there, she said, "Emma, since it's a white school, maybe I'm not allowed on the playground."

I hadn't thought about that, and I reckon Mrs. Fleury hadn't either.

Just then Lullah spied Oralee and Lily on the swings.

"We can stand across the street and I'll yell to them," she said. "Maybe they'll come over and we can go play somewhere else."

Lullah waved so hard it didn't take the girls long to see her. Oralee waved back and beckoned for Lullah to come over.

Lullah just shook her head and called, "Let's go play somewhere else. Let's play hide-and-seek in the cane field near here."

Lily Michot began pumping higher and higher and squealing like she was having a wonderful time. Oralee looked at her flying up in the air like a bird.

"It's more fun swinging," she yelled back. "We don't want to play in the old scratchy cane."

"I've got to hurry and meet Eula Mae," I told Lullah.

"I'm going to wait here a while," Lullah said. "Maybe they'll get tired of swinging."

So I left her there and the last I saw, Lullah was squatting on the sidewalk just looking across at the other two swinging.

When I got home from Belltown that evening I asked Lullah, "Did the girls ever go play with you?"

"No," Lullah said. "I watched them having fun for a while. Then I came home."

6

The Picnic in the Cemetery

Sugarcane harvest began the last of October. That's always a busy, exciting time. We don't see much of Daddy Jobe once the cutting starts. He drives the great big cane cutter and sometimes the tractor that pulls the cane wagons to the mill.

But before anything starts, Father Austin goes out in the field with a couple of altar boys and blesses the crops for Mr. Arnaud.

It's a right pretty sight, and a lot of folks go to see it. I was still on vacation, but Lullah couldn't go along because she was back in the public school for colored children again.

Mama and me and Little Jobe walked over to the field to watch. The cane was higher than our heads, thick and green as grass. All the machinery was lined up for the blessing, and Rubie Johnson even drove over his pair of mules.

Father Austin came in his good lace surplice, and two altar boys with him. It looked like a real jubilee.

Father said the blessing in a loud voice to come from a little short man. It's such a pretty prayer I can remember parts of it by heart like I do the catechism answers.

"Almighty, everlasting God, who by Thy word didst create the heavens, the earth, the sea and all the things visible and invisible. . . ."

It made me feel like I was made special by God and real important to Him even if I was just a scrub girl.

"Who didst command the earth to bring forth the plants and trees, each bearing fruit according to its own seed for the use of men and animals."

That helped us know He had made the sugarcane for us so we could make a living out of it, and have sugar for our coffee and molasses on our pancakes.

"Pour into them over and above the natural power with which Thou didst endow them the grace of Thy new blessing."

We knew that God had really blessed us with a bumper crop that would have lots of sugar in the syrup.

Father Austin sprinkled holy water toward the cane and the machines and Rubie Johnson's mules.

Then they started up the cane cutter, and Daddy Jobe cut the first heap. That's what we call three rows. There are knives in front of the machine that do the cutting. The stalks ride all the way around the cutter and fall off in a pile on the other side. It's something to see.

Daddy Jobe looked so high and mighty up there driving the big cane cutter and making it go wherever he wanted. We sure felt proud of him. Why, he could have turned that machine around and mowed us all down. He had that much power.

We went home by way of the Bethel Church in the country. It's a pretty little frame church with an old plantation bell set in a frame on the ground. The folks who go there sure do keep their church up. It was painted white as hand-picked cotton, and so were many of the tombs and headstones in the Resurrection Cemetery beside it.

"If I'd thought," Mama said, "we could have brought some food and had us a picnic in the cemetery. It's such a warm fall day."

We often have picnics there because there's grass and shade and it's real pretty.

That gave me the idea for something to bring Lullah and Oralee back together. I'd fix up a nice basket of food and take the children for a picnic out in the cemetery come Saturday. I could get Essie Jones to take my place at the motel for a couple of hours.

Lullah was real happy at my idea. She hurried off to invite Oralee. She came back looking half happy.

"Oralee can come," she said, "but she asked if she couldn't bring Lily Michot too. So I had to be polite and tell her Yes."

But Lullah was lighthearted as a hummingbird Saturday morning when we got busy making the picnic lunch. Mama fried the chicken because there's nobody can do it as good as she can. I baked a sweet potato pie because that's Oralee's favorite.

Lullah helped me squeeze lemons for the lemonade, and that's a messy job. It's even messier when Little Jobe tries to help.

Oralee and Lily were to meet us at the corner of Mr. Arnaud's south field. It was such a warm day we didn't even need our sweaters. Lullah carried the pail of lemonade and I had the basket of food on my arm.

Little Jobe pranced behind us half singing, "Chick-a-la-bye, chick-a-la-bye. Give me your toe and I'll make you a pie."

The white gravel alongside the road was dirtied with torn leaves fallen from the cane wagons. And we had to watch out because there were so many wagons going by. They were hooked one behind another with a truck pulling them. And the stalks were piled so high, you'd think they would upset.

We could see gray smoke over some of the fields where they were burning off the leaves before they sent the stalks to the co-op mill. And the smell of raw cane juice was in the air thick as the smoke.

The eleven-thirty whistle blew at the mill across the fields. Then a truck slowed down beside us and stopped. Daddy Jobe leaned out.

"You children want to go through the mill?" he asked. "Little Jobe's never been there."

We explained we were on our way to have a picnic.

Right off Little Jobe cried, "I want to go to the sugar mill and have the picnic there."

"It's already been set that we're going to the cemetery," I told him. "If you want to go to the mill with Daddy, you just won't get any picnic."

"I'll take you another time," Daddy Jobe promised him. So that settled it.

Down by the bayou path a nosey old hound dog joined up with us. He kept sniffing at the basket and I kept telling him to go on home.

"Why do dogs always sniff at everything?" Little Jobe asked.

"It's because way back a long time ago," I told him, "all the dogs got together to have a big feast. They brought bones and gizzards and grease and salt and pepper to cook them up a fine gumbo. Then when it came time to put in the pepper, it was gone. Somebody had stolen it. The dogs ran around sniffing each other, but they couldn't find the guilty one. So ever since then, all the dogs sniff at everybody and everything to find the stolen pepper. Daddy Jobe told me that when I was little as you."

"Is it true?" Lullah asked.

Little Jobe gave the hound a shove and said, "Go 'way! We ain't got your pepper."

The dog looked real disappointed. Then he turned his tail around and ran off.

"See!" I said to Lullah. "It must be true."

Oralee and Lily were already waiting for us. Oralee was pleasant as pie, and she'd put on a new flowered cotton dress for the picnic.

Lily Michot is a nervous little girl who bites her lip and keeps running her round comb through her long black hair. But she's always clean as a pin.

It sure was nice in the Resurrection Cemetery. The grass was still green, and the church people had kept it mowed. The pine trees made such good shade that we set the lemonade pail under one to keep it cool.

The children went running around reading the names on the gravestones. And I warned Little Jobe that he wasn't to go near the church because I had a feeling he would try ringing that bell if he got half a chance.

"Look! Here's Margaret Howard lived to be a hundred and two," said Oralee in a wondering voice.

"Come here," called Lullah. "This poor little Zero Jackson died when he was only three days old."

But I began noticing that Oralee and Lily were keeping together and not paying attention to anything Lullah told them about. They went running off to an old brick tomb that was toppled over inside a rusted iron fence.

I picked out the Simmons' family tomb for a table because it was wide and low. It was so clean and white we really didn't need a tablecloth, but I spread ours over it out of respect for the Simmonses.

Oralee and Lily came back and stood watching Lullah and me setting out the plates and covered dishes.

"I like the nice hot lunches we get at school, don't you?" Lily asked Oralee.

"We had to bring our own at St. Joseph's," said Oralee.

"We always have hot food at our public school too," Lullah put in as she set down a jar of pickles.

"Poor little Lullah!" Lily said, looking sad as a crocodile. "It's too bad you can't go to school with us."

Lullah's bottom lip pushed out. "I don't want to go to your old school," she said. "I wouldn't go if they paid me ten dollars."

It went on that way and I could see Lullah was brewing up a storm inside.

"What are you so sour about today?" Oralee asked her. "You got a gravel in your shoe or something?"

"If I have, it's not hurting your foot," Lullah said back.

I thought it was time to butt in. "Will you fetch the lemonade, Lullah?" I asked. "Everything's about ready."

Lullah went to the tree and leaned over the pail. She stamped her foot. "Darn this old tree!" she said. "Some pine needles dropped into the lemonade."

Little Jobe started whining, "I don't want pine needles in my lemonade."

"Shut up, boy!" cried Lullah. She was really mad.

Oralee began dancing around her and singsonging, "Lullah's mad and I am glad and I know what will please her, some lemonade with piney needles and three little monkeys to squeeze her."

Then the storm broke. Lightning flashed in Lullah's eyes. She swung the pail and threw the lemonade over Oralee. Then she kicked it across the grass.

Oralee acted like she was drowning. She gasped and spluttered. Then she yelled, "I hate you, Lullah Royall. I'll never speak to you again."

She went running over the graves to the road. Lily stood biting her lip and looking at the picnic lunch set out so nice. Then she combed back her hair and followed Oralee.

I ran out into the road and called, "Come back, Oralee! We haven't eaten our picnic yet. And there's sweet potato pie for dessert."

But she never looked back once.

Little Jobe began bawling. "I want some lemonade. I helped make it and I didn't get none."

That broke a storm in me. "If there was a cupful left, boy," I yelled at him, "I'd give it to you the same way Oralee got it."

Lullah was heaped on the ground crying her heart out on the grass. "I wish I was dead," she sobbed. "I wish I was inside one of these tombs. I wish I hadn't thrown the lemonade on Oralee."

"She was asking for it." I tried to comfort her. "Now she can be sour for a while."

Lullah wouldn't touch a bite of the food, and I just pecked at the chicken. But Little Jobe made up for both of us. I never saw a boy stuff so much inside him. Then he started whining about the lemonade again.

7

The Sugar Mill

One night Daddy Jobe called us to the window to look at the moon. It was bright yellow and sitting on top of the sugarcane.

"Never saw the moon so close before," Daddy said. "Little Jobe, you want me to put some molasses on your fingers and take you out in the field to catch the moon?"

Little Jobe pushed his nose against the glass. Then he said, "No, I want you to take me to the mill and show me that big brown mountain of sugar."

We had to laugh. Ever since Little Jobe heard Daddy talk about how the raw sugar was heaped in a mountain inside the mill, he'd been teasing to see it.

"All right," Daddy Jobe said. "You and Emma meet me at Mr. Arnaud's field derrick tomorrow morning and you can ride to the mill on the truck with me."

It would be my day off, so I was glad to go. Lullah was interested too, but she had to go to school.

The derrick is right near the highway. The trucks bring the burned-off cane there, and the big derrick lifts it out and piles it on the ground. Later the derrick raises it into the empty cane wagons that are waiting to take it to the mill.

You might know how surprised I was when we got there and found Lullah waiting for us.

"You're playing hooky, girl," I told her.

She grinned at me. "I don't feel like going to school today," she said. "I'd rather go through the mill again because I'm not so crazy about school anymore."

"Maybe you've earned a holiday," I said. "You've been pretty steady about school up to now."

We stood and watched while Daddy Jobe drove the truck to pull a long cable working the derrick. That daddy of ours can drive anything that runs with an engine—and mules too, I reckon.

While we were riding to the mill he first scolded Lullah for playing hooky. "You don't know how lucky you are, girl," he said. "You should have seen the tumble-down school I went to when I was your age, and it didn't go past sixth grade."

Then he told us about the old times in cane harvesting when they didn't use machines. "It was hard work because we cut all the cane by hand," he told us. "But it was more fun because everybody turned out to work in the fields."

"I wish I'd lived then," I said. "I'd be a field hand instead of a scrub girl."

"You would have worked harder and got less money," Daddy Jobe said.

"Tell us more," begged Lullah. "Didn't you bring the cane in from the fields with mules and wagons like Rubie Johnson still uses?"

"Mostly," said Daddy Jobe. "But they did have little trains on the bigger plantations, and one year I drove the little dingy engine. Then when the harvest was over, the whistle would blow and we'd have a big party with a bonfire of cane tops big as a burning mountain. And there would be a barbecue with dancing and singing. And of course we had plenty of cane juice to drink."

"I want to drink cane juice," said Little Jobe. "Please, Daddy, I want some cane juice."

Daddy Jobe looked down at him and said, "We don't

have that kind of parties anymore, but I'll get you some cane to chew."

He turned the truck out on the white gravel and stopped there. He picked up a knife with a broad blade from behind the seat. He whacked off a stalk growing in the field. He peeled it and cut it into three equal pieces.

Then Daddy Jobe jumped back into the truck and gave us each a piece. "Here's your cane juice," he said. "You got to chew it out."

Lullah and I had chewed cane before so it wasn't much of a treat. It's tough and full of stringy little sticks, and you have to bite them together to squeeze out any juice.

But Little Jobe thought he was having an old-time feast. And I think he was chewing up the sticks too, and swallowing them.

By that time we got to the mill. It's a great big white building with tall chimneys. A lot of cane wagons were lined up outside waiting their turn to dump their loads into the carrier. We could see the stalks riding up into the mill.

Daddy Jobe led us up some steps so we could see the cane getting cut by whirling knives. The juice was coming out of it in a flood.

The place was full of noises and smells. We had to

climb steep stairs to the big steel platforms.

"You keep an eye on Little Jobe," Daddy yelled into my ear. That boy was trying to climb up everywhere and look into everything.

"When we going to see the sugar mountain?" he kept yelling up at Daddy Jobe and the rest of us. You had to yell to be heard in that place.

There are machines to clean the juice, and tanks that cook the water out as it thickens into syrup. And there are pipes and pulleys running everywhere.

I always did like the vacuum tank where the sugar starts coming out in the molasses, and I wish I had one home in our kitchen. Mr. Roche opened a valve thing and smeared our fingers with some of it. Then he had us look through a magnifying glass to see the sugar. It looks like gold sand in the molasses.

But Little Jobe kept after us until we went down the stairs and into the shed at the side of the mill. There was that big mountain of sugar piled all the way to the roof. It would go off to the refinery later, Mr. Roche told us. "All the impurities and molasses left will be taken out," he said, "and that will leave pure white sugar like you got on your table."

Daddy Jobe let us each take a pinch to taste, like we

always do. Then he and Mr. Roche began talking about crops and what good sugar they were getting. It wasn't so noisy in the shed, so they could talk better.

Me and Lullah went and stood in the doorway to rest our ears and noses.

Next thing we knew, Little Jobe was yelling, "Look at me, everybody! Everybody look at me! I'm standing on top of the world."

He had climbed to the top of all that sugar and was half sunk into it. Sugar was sprinkled over his head and shoulders so thick that he looked like a molasses pie.

"You get down out of that sugar," Daddy Jobe shouted to him. "You come down here right away."

Little Jobe came sliding down the mountain like he was on a sled. "Whe-e-e-e!" he yelled.

And was he a mess! His hair and clothes were full of raw sugar, and it clings bad as cobwebs.

Daddy Jobe tried to wash off his arms and legs with a hose. But the water was so cold that Little Jobe howled and squirmed so he got wet all over. Then he was sticky as if he had fallen into a tank of molasses.

Daddy shook his finger at him. I reckon he wanted to whip him but that would get him all sticky too. "I declare you're the worst boy in this parish," Daddy Jobe told him. "And why didn't you watch him like I told you?" he scolded me.

He was the maddest at us I've ever seen him get.

Then he told me, "You take that boy right home! And walk there. Don't take him anywhere near my truck."

So Lullah and I started out with Little Jobe following us and sucking his fingers.

"You're sure a lollipop," Lullah said to him.

But he didn't care at all. He'd just reached into his pocket and found it was full of sugar.

"You're going to get sick," I warned him, "if you don't quit eating that sugar."

But I was so mad at him that I didn't much care if he did.

As we passed the entrance to Azalie I saw two little girls walking down the lane. Lullah saw them too, and it didn't take any guessing to know Oralee's reddish plait and Lily Michot's long black hair. We knew they were playing hooky too. Each one had a shovel, so we knew why. I reckon it brought back happier times to Lullah. She lowered her head and began kicking the gravel at every step.

Next thing happened, Little Jobe was so busy picking sugar out of his pocket, he stumbled over a rock and fell into the ditch. When he climbed out of there, he really was a sight with all the gravel and leaves stuck to him. He looked like something awful that had come out of the swamp.

We just stood off from the house and called Mama when we got home. She came out on the porch, and Little Jobe cried so proudfully, "I climbed the sugar mountain. I climbed clear to the top."

"Don't come any closer," Mama yelled at him. "Stay right where you are. You girls help me fill a tub from the cistern. I'll bring it outside."

She was so upset she didn't think about how Lullah should have been at school.

Little Jobe began squalling some more when we pulled off his clothes and dumped him into the tub. The cistern water was cold as what came out of the hose, I reckon. Mama didn't even take time to heat it. Then she dried him with a towel and hustled him inside to get some clean clothes.

It wasn't until she finished with Little Jobe that she said to Lullah, "How come you aren't at school?"

Then Lullah began saying her stomach had been aching her again. But I could see Mama didn't believe her although she gave her a dose of baking soda in water.

Daddy Jobe came home that night still mad. He wouldn't even talk to us. Not until Little Jobe began begging, "I want to put 'lasses on my fingers tonight and go catch the moon. Can I, Daddy? Can I?"

Daddy Jobe grabbed him by the shoulders and gave him a hard shake. "Boy, don't you ever let me see you with sticky fingers again," he scolded, "or you'll catch something besides the moon."

8

Uncle Vounie

I was out in the garden picking mustard greens. We always plant them in the fall because it's too hot for them to be growing in the summer. The same with turnip greens and lettuce.

Lullah came hopscotching across the rows and squatted down beside me. She began helping pick, but I could see her mind wasn't on mustard greens.

"Emma," she said, "I've been thinking I did a mean thing when I threw that lemonade on Oralee. I've been thinking maybe I ought to apologize to her. Sure cut me to see her go treasure digging with Lily Michot."

"Humph!" I said back. "She ought to apologize too. She didn't act like any sweet jasmine on the picnic."

"But somebody's got to be first," Lullah said.

"And I've got a feeling it's going to be you," I told her.

Lullah began chewing a leaf. I could see she was still studying over it.

"Oralee's birthday is Saturday," she said, "and I could take her over a present and make up with her then."

"Uh-huh!" I said. "That's just like you. You always were softhearted." Then I had to give in. "But you're not the only softhearted one. I'm thinking I might buy you a nice fifty-cent box of candy to give Oralee."

Lullah began picking the greens twice as fast. "Oh, Emma, you will? You will?" she cried. "You're the best sister in the whole world."

"Too bad I'm not your best friend," I said. Maybe I was always a little jealous of Oralee.

Anyway, the next day I went to the superette. I bought a box of chocolates all tied up in pink ribbons and shiny paper. And it cost me a dollar instead of fifty cents.

But I sure said the wrong thing when I gave it to Lullah. "I saw old Uncle Vounie in town," I told her. "You ought to go see him and get some old-time love potion to put in this candy."

I was just joking but Lullah took it real seriously.

"Oh, Emma," she cried, "will you take me back in the swamp to see him? Will you? Please! Please!"

"No, I won't do such foolishness," I said.

"Please, Emma." She kept at me. "You've been fishing with Daddy Jobe down the bayou near the swamp and you know how to get there."

She was after me worse than Little Jobe, so at last I gave in. There's only one reason I let her beg me into such a foolish thing. I began thinking that maybe we could do some fishing on the way back and get a nice mess of perch for supper.

I went to see Eula Mae and asked her how to get to Uncle Vounie's once you rowed into the swamp.

Then Lullah and me set off with the old cane pole. We took the path to the bayou and began looking for Mr. Arnaud's pirogue. He leaves it on the bank for anybody to use. That's how Daddy Jobe and me go fishing sometimes. It would be just right in the swamp because they say you can float a pirogue on a puddle.

It was there, and the paddle too. I was afraid some boys might have gone off with them.

The bayou is like a long canal. It's full of water hyacinths in some places, and wild cane and willows grow on the banks. When you get down it a piece, there's a big dead tree lies across a creek. It's all hung with long moss like a curtain. Once you lift the moss and go up the creek, you're in the swamp.

"It's sure spooky in here," I said.

I could see Lullah was starting to get afraid. She sat there in that long, narrow boat with her sweater pulled tight around her so snakes couldn't drop off the trees down her neck. She kept staring down at the water.

Everything was quiet and ghosty. The water was dirty brown and half covered with green scum. Cypress trees huddled together with their knees pulled up out of the water. The black snags sticking out of the slime looked like alligator heads.

I paddled the boat through the stagnant water and under the cypress trees. A flock of buzzards were perching on a bare tree ahead just waiting, waiting for something to die—maybe us.

Lullah kept scrooching lower and lower in the boat.

"You sure you want to go on, girl?" I asked her. "We could turn around and go fishing in the bayou."

But Lullah nodded her head and pulled her sweater tighter around her.

So I paddled around a floating island the way Eula Mae had told me until I could see an old shanty built up on a wooden platform. That would be Uncle Vounie's place.

As we got closer we could see spiderlike roots laid out to dry on the boards. There were some gourd dippers hanging by the door, and smoke was coming out of the crazy chimney.

We went up alongside the platform and I steadied the boat while Lullah climbed out. I tied the pirogue to a post and got out too.

Suddenly I thought the swamp devil was after us for sure. There was a swoosh of wind and a horrible squawking over our heads. A black shadow crossed us, and a great big thing swooped down at Lullah and me. She screamed and I almost fell into the water.

Then we saw it was a big blue heron. He landed on the platform and came walking to us like he was on stilts. "Kwak, kwak," he squawked deeper down his throat than Daddy Jobe.

"Hey, you Geechee!" yelled a cracked voice from the rickety shanty. "You bad Geechee!"

There stood Uncle Vounie in overalls with a woman's sunbonnet on his head. His face under the bonnet looked like a popped cotton boll with his dry, brown skin and fluffy white beard.

"Don't you pay him any mind," Uncle Vounie said. "That's just my pet heron, Geechee. I saved him from a snapping turtle when he was a baby and fell out of his nest."

I looked at his pet again and had to laugh. Geechee looked more comical than fearsome with his skinny head and neck and skinny legs and toes. He was almost tall as Lullah, and he kept looking us over like a curious old man.

"Welcome, children," Uncle Vounie said. "Come inside and set."

Lullah held back. She looked scared of Uncle Vounie. So I took her by the hand and led her in.

It was a right poor-looking room with an old tumbledown bed and some rickety chairs. There were bunches of herbs drying on the wall. But the most noticeable thing was a big black pot of something boiling on the wood stove. It smelled like old swamp water.

"Now what misery you got?" Uncle Vounie asked. "You're too young for rheumatiz and too old for colic."

Lullah looked so shy and scared I knew she'd never tell him what she wanted, so I talked for her.

"My little sister Lullah here wants to get a love potion," I told him, and I sure felt silly.

Uncle Vounie looked at her and his face cracked in a grin.

"Ain't you kind of young to be looking for a husband?" he asked.

"It's not a husband," I explained. "It's to give her best friend in a box of candy. They had a squabble and Oralee won't play with her anymore."

"Now that's too bad," Uncle Vounie said. "I sure wish there was a root for that."

"But Oralee and some of the other children said you're a powerful hoodoo man," Lullah said. I reckon being so disappointed set her tongue loose.

Uncle Vounie laughed and laughed in a way that sounded like ice cracking up.

"Then don't tell them I ain't," he said. "Wouldn't want to spoil their fun."

"Can't you even make love potions?" asked Lullah, looking at the pot boiling on the stove.

"I'm no hoodoo man, little girl," Uncle Vounie said. "I'm just an old remedy man cooks up medicine to heal sick folks. If it's hoodoo you want, you'll have to do it yourself."

Lullah's head hung like the bait on a fishing pole.

"We're much obliged," I mumbled to Uncle Vounie.

"I reckon we better go now. We've got fishing to do."

He and that skinny bird followed us to the boat. Uncle Vounie helped us get in and untied the rope.

As we drifted off he put his hands to his mouth and yelled across the water, "Hoodoo? You do. I don't. You do." Little Jobe sure would have liked that little sing-song.

I paddled us back through the swamp to the bayou. Everything seemed more alive. The buzzards had left the tree and were flying round and round high in the sky as if they had given up waiting for us. A turtle went sliding into the water beside our boat. Two gray squirrels ran through the branches of a cypress tree and chuck-chucked at us.

"That Uncle Vounie," said Lullah. "He's just a fake."

"We sure wasted our time," I told her back. "We should have gone fishing in the first place."

9

Oralee's Birthday

Before I left for the motel, I said to Lullah, "Now when you go to see Oralee today, don't give her that box of candy until she makes up with you. I paid a whole dollar for it, and I don't want to see it wasted."

We had kind of a slow day for a Saturday. Some men had come for the rabbit hunting, and there was a traveling salesman in Number Five but he left early. So there wasn't so much cleaning to be done until Sunday. That's why Mrs. Lepine let me off early.

Lullah was waiting for me at home with the box of candy.

"So she wouldn't make up with you," I said. "I'm sure glad you didn't give her the candy."

"I haven't gone yet," Lullah told me. "I've been waiting for you to get back. I'm sure glad you're early."

"What have I got to do with it?" I asked her suspiciously. "I've already bought the candy."

Lullah smoothed out the pink bow. "I've been thinking maybe you'd go with me," she said. "You could help me explain."

I was out of patience with her. "Girl, can't you do anything for yourself?" I asked. "Besides, I went with you to Uncle Vounie's, and what good did it do?"

"But this is different," Lullah said. She threw her arms around me. "Please, pretty please, Emma," she begged. "You're the best sister I've got in the world."

"I'm the only sister you've got," I said.

"And I'm the only little sister you've got," she went on in such a pitiful way. "If I were to die tomorrow, you wouldn't have one."

Nobody can stand up long against Lullah's coaxing. Nobody but Mama. She would have said to her, "Save that sweet talk for your friend Oralee. You'll need it because I'm not going, and I don't think it's going to kill you."

But I'm not Mama. So I said, "Oh, all right. I'll go there with you this once, but I don't promise what I'm going say to that trifling girl."

"Oh, you won't say anything mean to Oralee, will you?" she asked me in a shocked voice.

"I might," I threatened her. "But most likely I won't say a single word, so there's really no good of me going."

I'd already made up my mind she'd have to do her own talking because it was none of my business.

We started down the road, with Lullah holding the candy box tight. It was another of those nice fall days with the sun warm on our heads.

Many of the cane fields we passed had already been cut and the next year's crop planted. Daddy Jobe had helped do that too. They lay stalks of old cane in trenches dug in the fields. Then they cover them over with dirt, and the new plants grow out of the joints of the buried cane.

French Grove looked the same as ever. So did the people, but the way they acted was different. Mrs. Tessin coming from town stared right through us like we were two windows. And Mrs. Benoit out sweeping her walk swept harder as we went by so the dirt flew over us. Lullah quickly tried to cover the box of candy with part of her skirt so it wouldn't get dirty. It made us feel like cane borers or some other pests.

Everything looked deserted at Oralee's house.

"Maybe she's not home again," said Lullah in a disappointed voice. She wiped the candy box once more to make sure it was clean. "Maybe she's gone off to the public school grounds with Lily Michot."

As we started up the walk I heard a lot of children's voices inside the screen door. I quickly grabbed Lullah and pulled her down in back of a holly bush with me.

We were just in time because the door opened and a flock of white girls came running out, Oralee among them. They were dressed in fancy ribbons and ruffles.

"It's a birthday party," Lullah whispered to me. "She's having a birthday party and she didn't invite me."

The girls went skipping and yelling around trying to decide what game to play.

"Let's play blindman's bluff," one of them cried. "That's a lot of fun."

"No, we played that at school yesterday," said another. It was Lily Michot. "Let's play hide-and-seek. Not it!"

"Not it!"

"Not it!"

"You're it, Oralee," cried Shirley Benoit.

Oralee went to one of the magnolia trees and put her face against the trunk. She began counting, "One, two, three, four . . ."

Then Lullah and I had a real fright. The girls began chasing around to find good hiding places. Some went behind the trees, and a couple around the house. But Lily and Myrtle Turnbuckle started toward the holly bushes.

Lily suddenly stopped, turned, and pointed to the porch steps. They both went running fast toward them. They disappeared behind the steps.

"Ready or not, here I come," called Oralee.

It didn't take her any time to find the girls behind the trees, but two of them got in free. Then, goodness me, Oralee started coming to look behind the holly bushes. But she heard Lily and another girl running across the grass, so she hurried back to try to get to the tree first.

Lullah began wriggling. "I've got an idea," she whispered to me. "I've got a great idea."

Oralee went to look behind the house. Then Lullah stood up and stepped away from the bush. She went racing across the yard to the tree and slapped it.

"Free!" she cried.

She turned around to the others. Oralee came running back and went over to Lullah. I could see she was laughing. She knew it was a good joke, and Oralee always did like a funny surprise.

"Happy birthday," Lullah said to her.

I think Oralee would have made up with Lullah ther and there and asked her to stay for the rest of the party

But Lily yelled at Lullah, "You've got no busines here. You weren't invited."

"Yeah!" Myrtle said. "Who invited you?"

I saw Lullah look pleadingly at Oralee. But Oralee jus stood there and hung her head.

I thought it was time to speak my piece. I came fro behind the bush and called, "Come on, Lullah. We'v got to hurry if we want to get to that party down th road."

Lullah waited a little while, but Oralee still stoc there looking ashamed and saying nothing. So Lulla came running down the walk to me. She took my har and started to turn back home, but I yanked her on.

"We're supposed to be going the other way," I wh pered to her. "Haven't you got pride?"

I hustled her away fast because I could hear the so coming up in her throat. She walked down the road, cı

ing into her hands and stumbling over the gravel. I sure felt for her.

"Oralee's not the only person in the world," I told her. "There's me and Little Jobe and lots of children besides those at the party."

After a little, her sobs got jerkier and farther apart. She wiped her eyes off on her sweater. She began scuffing the gravel and I could see she was thinking hard.

"Reckon I've been a plain fool, Emma," she said when we got a ways down the road, "and you're right. I've got lots of friends like you all and Sister Rosalie and Father Austin. I'm going back to St. Joseph's School. Little Jobe sure was broken up when I quit."

"Now you're talking sense," I said, "and if I hadn't lost so many years, I'd go with you."

"I can go back alone," said Lullah. "I don't mind if I'm the only one there. It won't be so empty for Sister Rosalie and Father Austin anyhow."

She seemed more content then. "I'm sure glad we still got this box of chocolates," she went on. "Let's find a nice place and sit down and eat them."

We began looking around. We were near the bayou, so we decided to go up the path and sit on the bank. The grass was real green there yet, and I found a nice sunny spot.

"Let's have the party," I said.

Lullah carefully worked the pink ribbon off the box.

"Let me tie the bow in your hair," she said.

"Shucks!" I said. "I don't have enough hair to hold a bow."

But she fastened it into my short hair as best she could. "You look pretty," she said, squinting her eyes at me. "You ought to buy some of those fancy barrettes and bows at the superette, then you won't look so much like a boy."

I was taking off the paper and opening the box. I picked out a fat raisin piece. Then I passed the box to her. "Happy birthday, Lullah," I said for fun.

She began pinching the chocolates to find a hard one. Then she passed the box back to me.

"Happy birthday, Emma," she came back at me.

"Stop pinching that candy," I fussed. "You're spoiling all the soft ones. Happy birthday yourself."

"We can save them for Little Jobe," she said. "He won't mind. Happy birthday for Little Jobe."

A blue shrimp boat with the name *Creole* painted on it came chugging by. Nets were hanging from the boom like big lace shawls. There was a man standing on the deck.

We waved to him and he waved back.

CREOLE
NEW ORLEANS

"Happy birthday, Mr. Creole," Lullah yelled. She held out the box. "Have a chocolate."

Then we laughed so much we just rolled in the grass. And the bow came out of my hair.

We hadn't acted so silly in a long time—or had more fun.

10

Mr. Buzzard Returns

Lullah said that when she suddenly showed up at St. Joseph's after the school had been empty so long, it must have seemed to the sisters that they were seeing a vision.

"When I marched into the fifth grade room," she told us, "Sister Rosalie looked like she couldn't believe her own eyes—not even with her glasses."

Lullah said she just looked up from her desk and kept staring at her. Then she took her glasses off and wiped them.

"Good morning, ma'am—I mean Sister," Lullah said. When you get used to talking to the teachers in public school, it's hard to remember to call a sister the right thing.

"Good morning, Lullah," Sister Rosalie said. "Have you come back for something you forgot?"

"No, Sister," Lullah answered her. "I've come to school. Shall I sit in my old place?"

Sister asked her, "Wouldn't you rather sit in front now that there are vacant seats there?"

So Lullah sat down in the front row and they said the morning rosary. Then Sister Rosalie took out the arithmetic book.

"Now where were we our last lesson?" she asked.

"We were studying fractions," Lullah answered, "and now I can add and subtract them."

"Good. Then we'll review fractions this morning," Sister decided.

Mama said, "Seems like she had enough time sitting in that empty school day after day to remember where you left off."

"Oh, they only kept the school open an hour each morning since nobody came," Lullah said. "Sister told me so, and that she spent the hour at her desk studying ancient history. I thought teachers knew all the history there ever was."

Lullah sure was happy going back to the parochial school.

"It's just like having my own private school and teacher," she said, "but I sure wish some of the others would come back."

I knew she meant Oralee, in spite of how that girl had treated her.

One time we thought there had been another bomb scare because she came home at noon.

"I'm learning so fast that Sister Rosalie says I only have to come in the mornings," she explained. "Reckon she doesn't want me to get too far ahead of the rest."

So Lullah started coming home soon after the mill whistle blew at eleven thirty. That was quitting time for morning in the cane fields too. And you should have seen all the books she brought with her. She studied them too.

"I'm at the head of my class," she joked.

"You're at the bottom too," I reminded her, because that's where I had usually been.

One time she seemed real upset when she got home. She led me aside and explained why. "Sister Rosalie and me heard footsteps in the hall," she said. "But they stopped at the stairs. She told me to go see was it somebody looking for Father Austin."

"But when I went down, there was nobody in the hall. So I went to the door and looked out. I saw a man walking away real fast. You know, Emma, I only saw that man's back but I could swear it was Mr. Buzzard."

"Now, Lullah," I told her, "it couldn't be him. He checked out of the motel long ago." I'd almost forgotten him. "Did he have a red face?"

"I couldn't see it," Lullah said. "It was only his back I saw."

"Was he flat-headed?" I asked.

"I don't know," she said. "He had a hat on."

"Then why you do think it was Mr. Buzzard?"

"I just feel it in my bones."

"Then don't tell Mama and Daddy Jobe," I warned her, "if you're not sure and only your bones think so. No use getting them all stirred up about nothing."

I really didn't believe the man was Mr. Buzzard. Probably somebody looking for Father Austin like Sister Rosalie thought.

Then one day we went to gather pecans from Mr. Arnaud's big tree out in his cow pasture. He told Daddy Jobe we could have them because he didn't have time to fool around with them. And he knows Mama makes the best pralines and pecan pies in the parish.

We got a big stick to knock down the nuts still in the tree. We put Mama's tin sieve upside down on Little

Jobe's head so he wouldn't get hurt by any falling nuts. And we brought one of the big water buckets.

Little Jobe ripped his overalls getting through the barbed wire fence, but they were old ones.

We went past the old sugar mill boiler set out in the field to hold water for the cows. Most of them were standing around with their jaws going like they were chewing gum.

First we picked up the nuts laying all over the ground. Then we took turns throwing the stick up in the tree to knock more loose.

Our bucket was almost full when we saw two men walking toward us. They had shotguns over their shoulders, and one of them was carrying a dead rabbit by the hind legs.

Glory, I could have fainted away when I saw it was Mr. Buzzard and Mr. 'Gator. They weren't at the motel, so they must have been hanging out in some town nearby, maybe Belltown.

They came straight at us, and we just stood there and gawked at them. When they got close, they stopped. Then Mr. Buzzard raised his shotgun and pointed it right at Lullah. He looked down the barrel and put his finger on the trigger.

Daddy Jobe hunts sometimes and he says, "Never point a gun at anything you don't want to kill." So I thought Lullah was a goner sure.

I'm plumb ashamed of myself to tell about it. I should have run in front of Lullah or something. But I was so scared my arms and legs wouldn't move.

Then Mr. Buzzard dropped his gun. He laughed his mean crow laugh. "Niggers scare easy," he said. "Let that be a lesson to you to stay away from St. Joseph's or you'll really get some buckshot next time."

He and Mr. 'Gator went on their way laughing. We just stood looking at them with open mouths like chickens with the gaps.

When they were clear past the water trough, Little Jobe grabbed up the stick and pointed it at them. "Bang, bang," he yelled so bravely.

We didn't gather any more pecans. We took what we had and hurried home to tell Mama.

When we finished telling her about it, she was looking like a rock had come through our window. She put her arms around Lullah and hugged her tight as if she was protecting her from Mr. Buzzard's gun.

"You better stop St. Joseph's, honey," she said. "That man's after you sure. He knows you're the only one went back."

Lullah hadn't cried or anything when the gun was pointed at her, but she sure made up for it now.

"I don't want to stop St. Joseph's," she sobbed. "I love that school, and Little Jobe wants to go there when he's big enough."

It just about tore me in two. I knew how much going to the school meant to her. So I butted in.

"Stopping school might not help much, Mama," I said, "if Mr. Buzzard's got it in for Lullah. He pointed the gun at her out in the field. Seems she's safer inside St. Joseph's. And I'll walk to school with her every morning if somebody will take her home at noon."

Lullah cried louder. "I love Sister Rosalie—and I'm head monitor and president of my class until the others come back," she cried. "If you'll let me go back, I'll never go out in the fields again."

Mama pulled at the bow on her *tignon* a couple times. Then she straightened her apron.

At last she said to Lullah, "I'll let you go back on one promise. You aren't to say a word about what happened today to your daddy. You know how he worries."

We promised we wouldn't. Daddy Jobe was having enough trouble with the cane cutter breaking down right in the middle of the harvest, let alone having Lullah to fret over too.

But it nearly got out at the supper table when Little Jobe said to Daddy, "I shot two bad men today."

Then Mama leaned across the table and shoved a hunk of bread into his open mouth.

"*Eat your supper,*" she said real cross.

11

The Shotgun Blast

When the ladies in Number Eight left me a fifty-cent tip, I said to myself, "Emma, this is your lucky day." I hadn't really done anything much for them—just picked up some bobby pins and curlers at the superette on my way to work.

It did seem like a lucky day to begin with. No torn sheets for me to mend or flooded floors from faucets left on. And we had had mostly clean tourists on their way to New Orleans.

Then about eleven o'clock Mrs. Lepine came hurrying to me with her face tight and her eyes squinting. "Now what's happened?" I thought to myself. "I know I dusted under the radiator in Number Six this time."

"Emma," Mrs. Lepine said, "I just had a phone call from Father Austin. Your sister's been shot at the school and they've got her at Dr. Bocage's."

Right off I started bawling. "Poor little Lullah! Is she going to die?"

"She's alive," said Mrs. Lepine. "That much I know. Now let's hope for the best unless we find out it's wrong."

As I followed her to the car I kept sobbing and saying over and over, "Poor little Lullah! Poor little Lullah!"

Mrs. Lepine started the engine and backed out of the motel. All the time I was crying up a storm into my best white handkerchief.

Mrs. Lepine's voice got sharp as usual. "Emma," she scolded me, "you're making me so nervous that I'll run into something sure."

So I hushed up as much as I could.

It's really not far from the Magnolia to French Grove, but it seemed far as New Orleans that morning. I kept saying my prayers over and over. And in between them I kept thinking of how I'd really been a little jealous of Lullah deep down in my heart because she was so pretty and smart. And I swore to myself I never would be again if only she wouldn't die.

At the doctor's house I jumped out of the car before it stopped and went running to his door. I never realized before how far back those houses sit from the road.

There's a sign on the door that says RING AND ENTER, but I just entered at a gallop.

Mama and Little Jobe were in the waiting room, watching for me. Mrs. Lepine came in behind me.

"Lullah's been bang-bang shot," Little Jobe cried.

"Lucky it was her ankle," Mama said, "and the pellets didn't go in too deep."

Then she rubbed her hand across her eyes like she wanted to shut something out of them.

Mrs. Lepine left as soon as she found out Lullah wasn't too bad off. Mama took me into the office, and there was Daddy Jobe looking like the end of the world had come. And little Lullah was sitting on the couch with Dr. Bocage bandaging up her ankle.

I made for Lullah right away. I rubbed her cheek with the back of my hand like Mama sometimes does to show us she loves us even if she doesn't talk about it.

"You all right now, honey?" I asked. "Does it hurt?"

I could feel her cheek was wet.

"It doesn't hurt so much now," she said.

I gave a side look at the little table near her and saw

the sharp knife and two bloody shotgun pellets lying on it. I knew it must have hurt awful for a while.

"She could have been shot dead," Daddy Jobe said. "She could just as easy have been shot dead." Then he put his face in his hands and acted like he had a cough.

"I never should have taken her to that school in the first place," I said.

"And I never should have let her go back when there was first talk about bombs," said Daddy Jobe.

"I'm worse to blame," said Mama. "Reckon I was too proud to keep her away from what was her right."

Dr. Bocage was having trouble tucking a piece of bandage under. He made a face like somebody was picking a shotgun pellet out of him.

"Don't talk nonsense," he said. "There are others more to blame than you all."

I reckon Little Jobe felt left out of everything. "My foot hurts," he began whining, but nobody listened to him at first.

"There now," Dr. Bocage said to Lullah, giving the bandage a little tap. "Keep off that ankle for a few days. We'll have some X rays made at the Belltown Hospital, but I'm sure I got all the shot."

Little Jobe began groaning, "My foot hurts. I want my foot wrapped up."

The doctor acted real serious about Little Jobe's foot then. He sat him on the couch beside Lullah. He fetched a flat stick and said, "Now open your mouth wide and say Ah."

If there's one thing Little Jobe can do, it's open his mouth like a bass.

"That's good," said Dr. Bocage. "I can see all the way to your toes. It looks pretty serious to me. You've caught appendicitis of the feet, little boy, but I've got the right medicine for that."

Somehow the doctor's joke loosened up all of us. Mama smiled and Daddy Jobe laughed out loud.

Dr. Bocage took a red lollipop out of a drawer and gave it to Little Jobe. That boy said another "Ah" and stuck it into his mouth.

Just then the doorbell began ringing real loud like somebody was dying. And without waiting, some men came tramping into the doctor's office. One was the sheriff. He looked like a soldier in his uniform with the pistol in his leather belt.

All of them knew Dr. Bocage, so they spoke a few polite things to him first. Then the sheriff got down to business and said, "I want the child's story of it."

He took the pad in his hand and wrote down the things Lullah told him. She had been on her way downstairs to get a book from the library for Sister Rosalie.

"We aren't supposed to run in the halls or on the stairs," she told him, "but I was in such a hurry to get the book that I sort of ran down the steps." She looked real ashamed.

"Then what?" asked the sheriff.

"Then there was a loud noise like when Daddy Jobe shoots at rabbits, and glass breaking, and something stung my ankle fierce."

"Have you any idea who fired the shotgun blast?" asked the sheriff.

"Yes, sir," Lullah said. "I'm sure it was Mr. Buzzard."

"Mr. Buzzard?" asked the sheriff. "Who's he?"

"He's Mr. 'Gator's friend," answered Lullah.

The sheriff twisted his mouth. "You've been reading too many animal stories, little girl," he said. "We want fact not fiction."

"That's true," I spoke up. "There were two mean men I named that. And one day out in the field Mr. Buzzard pointed a shotgun at Lullah and said she'd get worse if she didn't stay away from St. Joseph's."

The sheriff was writing that down.

"I shot them, bang-bang," cried Little Jobe, pulling the lollipop out of his mouth.

"We have a witness who says the man who fired the

shot fled in an old green sedan," said the sheriff, not paying any mind to Little Jobe.

Then I had a flash in the head. "That's them," I cried. "They stayed at the Magnolia last summer. Everybody who stops there has to register, so Mrs. Lepine must have their names and license number. She doesn't trust anybody."

"That's more help," he said. The sheriff was kind of like Mama because he didn't have much to say beside questions, and we couldn't tell what he was thinking. He gathered the two pellets into a piece of tissue Dr. Bocage gave him and stuffed them into his pocket.

No sooner had he gone with the other men than Father Austin came in.

"I'll drive all of you home," he told us.

I really should have gone back to the Magnolia, but I was too excited and upset to be any good for the rest of the day.

We rode home in Father Austin's car, and Mama was going to put Lullah to bed right away. But Lullah didn't want that. She went hopping and flopping around on one foot like the little lame sparrow that comes to our window for crumbs sometimes.

"I'll make you some cocoa, special," Mama said to Lullah.

"Can I get anything for you at the superette before I go back to the field, honey?" Daddy Jobe asked her. "How'd you like some ice cream or a picture book?"

I reached into my pocket. "Here's a fifty-cent piece some ladies gave me," I said to Lullah. "You can have it."

Then Little Jobe yelled, "My foot hurts and I want some peppermint candy and ice cream and pecan pie."

12

Visitors

Lullah sure was the Mardi Gras queen for the next few days. Seemed like all we did was answer the door and bring folks in to see her. Of course the sisters came and gave her a lot of sympathy and medals and holy cards. And Father Austin dropped by every day.

Mrs. Fleury was one of the first too. She brought Lullah a pretty handkerchief with rosebuds embroidered on it and told her how sorry she was about what had happened.

"How's Oralee?" Lullah asked politely.

"Just fine," said Mrs. Fleury. "She's coming to see you soon. I'll tell her you look fine too."

Lullah really looked kind of peaked and didn't pick up very well. The doctor said the X rays were okay and her ankle was doing good, but my little sister seemed to have lost her spirit.

Then one afternoon a car stopped beside the road and two ladies got out. Mrs. Cole was the first, and you could have knocked me over with a palm-leaf fan when I saw Mrs. Benoit following her. Both of them were dressed up in hats and gloves like they were going to make an elegant call.

"Come right in," Mama asked them, holding the door open. "Emma, you go drip some coffee right away."

But Mrs. Benoit quickly said, "We can't stay but a minute because we're on our way to our bridge club." So the hats and gloves weren't for us. They stood out on the porch and asked how Lullah was coming along. Then Mrs. Cole said, "They got the man that shot her."

"Heaven be praised!" Mama cried. "Who is he?"

"Somebody from across the state line," said Mrs. Cole. "Him and his sidekick. We heard that Hank Turnbuckle belongs to a secret society in Belltown and that they sent for the men to come and stir up the trouble."

"Did those two throw that rock through the Roches' window?" I asked.

"No, but they put the big boys up to it," said Mrs. Cole. "As if some of those boys can't get into enough mischief without any outside help."

"Did the boys make those phone calls too?" Mama wanted to know.

"No, it was the men," said Mrs. Cole, "and I don't doubt Hank was in it too. The sheriff was in the store and told me all about it."

"They were slippery as okra," Mrs. Benoit put in. "They had their nerve calling up and saying Mr. Benoit would lose his job at the mill."

"I sure hope they don't come back," Mama said.

"They won't," Mrs. Cole told her, "and I hear the Turnbuckles are moving away too. They know they aren't very popular here anymore. The awful thing they did to Lullah taught a lesson to some folks in French Grove."

Mrs. Benoit looked real pious and said, "It could just as easy have been a white child."

"Plenty of people are saying it could have been their own children," said Mrs. Cole.

Before they left, Mrs. Cole gave Mama a box of cookies from the store for Lullah. And she stuck her head in the door and said "Hello" and "Get well soon" to her.

"We're going to be late," said Mrs. Benoit looking at her wristwatch and tapping her shiny new shoe.

Soon as they left in Mrs. Benoit's car, Lullah asked Mama real anxiously, "Can't I go back to St. Joseph's now? I heard them telling how they've caught those bad men."

"I want to go to St. Joseph's," Little Jobe began whining. "You all said I could go to St. Joseph's."

"You'll go in time," Mama told him. "You'll go because your sister helped fix it so you could."

Lullah perked up right after that. I think she had been grieving inside because she thought St. Joseph's School had ended for her.

She looked real well the day a bunch of the children came to see her. Oralee was with them, squeezing a bouquet of holly full of red berries. They all looked big-eyed, and tiptoed in like they were coming to somebody's funeral.

Little Jobe dropped the sticks he was trying to build a cane wagon with and followed them in because he saw the girls had a box of candy.

Lullah was sitting in the rocking chair where Mama tried to keep her most of the time. Oralee handed her the bouquet and the girls gave her the candy.

"We're awful sorry about you getting shot," Oralee said. "Does it hurt bad?"

Then Lullah kind of rolled her eyes around and groaned a little for them. "It hurts awful sometimes," she said.

"Why, Lullah, you just been saying—" I started off, then I shut my mouth. I could see she wanted some sympathy from them, and I thought she had a right to it.

"How soon can you go back to school?" Oralee asked. "We're all going back to St. Joseph's now they've caught those bad men. That is, all of us here anyway."

Gussie Roman piped up, "Diana Tessin says she won't. Myrtle Turnbuckle's moving away. And Mrs. Thompson across the fields says she's not sending her boys, but she always ends up doing what everybody else does."

"And Lily's not going because she's always gone to public school," Oralee ended up. Then she twisted her fingers and looked down at the floor. "I would have come sooner to see you," she said, "but I was afraid you were real mad at me and wouldn't want to see me."

Lullah began rubbing the arm of the chair real hard like it had dust on it. "I never was mad at you, Oralee," she answered back, "except for the time I threw the lemonade on you, and I thought you had it coming."

"I'm sorry about that," Oralee kind of mumbled, and began pushing the toe of her shoe along the floor. "And about the birthday party—I really wanted you to stay."

"Seems like you could have said so *then,*" said Lullah, looking up at her, "but I wasn't mad at you."

The room got quiet as a church for a few moments, and the girls looked uneasy.

Then that little imp of a Jobe began singsonging, "Lullah's not mad and I'm glad and I know what will please her. A box of candy and Oralee to squeeze her. Let's open that candy now."

Everybody just hollered at that, and I think Lullah laughed hardest. That sure broke up the ice.

Oralee ran over to Lullah and gave her a big hug. "You're still my best friend, aren't you?" she asked, and I thought her eyes looked like morning glories at sunup.

"Sure," said Lullah. "Even best friends got to have squabbles now and then, I reckon. But we've sure had a lot of fun together most of the time."

"Like that day at Azalie when Little Jobe found the quarter and thought it was the plantation treasure," Oralee remembered with a giggle.

But Little Jobe was getting out of patience with their sweet talk. "I bought peppermint candy with it for all of us," he said to them, "so why can't Lullah hurry up and open that box and give me some of her candy?"

That set everybody laughing again and Lullah began untying the pretty red ribbon on the box. She handed it to Oralee. "You always did like red, so it's for you," she told her. "And remember the time we were both monitors at St. Joseph's and spilled the trash basket down the stairs when Father Austin was coming up them?"

All the girls giggled like they knew about it, but I'd never heard that one before.

Lullah passed the candy around, and it was like a real party. The girls forgot all about leaving for a long time. Then Gussie Roman said, "We've got to go now. Mama said we should only stay a few minutes, and I bet we've been here an hour already."

So they all told Lullah good-bye and started for the door, with Oralee the last to go.

"Get well soon, Lullah," they were all saying together.

And Oralee called back, "Looks like you'll have a lot of friends besides me when we go back to St. Joseph's."